P9-CRC-107

NICKELODEON

Drake & Josh

Kid Trouble

Kid Trouble

Adapted by Laurie McElroy
Based on "Little Sibling," written by Dan Schneider
and "Megan's New Teacher," written by George Doty IV.

Based on *Drake & Josh* created by Dan Schneider

SCHOLASTIC INC.
New York   Toronto   London   Auckland   Sydney
Mexico City   New Delhi   Hong Kong   Buenos Aires

If you purchased this book without a cover, you should be aware that this book is stolen property. It was reported as "unsold and destroyed" to the publisher, and neither the author nor the publisher has received any payment for this "stripped book."

No part of this work may be reproduced in whole or in part, stored in a retrieval system, or transmitted in any form or by any means, electronic, mechanical, photocopying, recording, or otherwise, without written permission of the publisher. For information regarding permission, write to Scholastic Inc., Attention: Permissions Department, 557 Broadway, New York, NY 10012.

ISBN-13: 978-0-439-89045-8
ISBN-10: 439-89045-4

© 2007 Viacom International Inc. All Rights Reserved.
Nickelodeon, Drake and Josh, and all related titles, logos, and characters are trademarks of Viacom International Inc.

Published by Scholastic Inc.

SCHOLASTIC and associated logos are trademarks and/or registered trademarks of Scholastic Inc.

12 11 10 9 8 7 6 5 4 3 2   7 8 9 10 11/0

Printed in the U.S.A.
First printing, January 2007

Kid Trouble

Part One
Little Sibling

PROLOGUE

Josh Nichols sat at the kitchen table after school with a bowl of nuts and a nutcracker. He cracked a big walnut, sending the shell flying. "You know what makes me feel good?" he asked with a smile. "Volunteering to help people."

Drake Parker, a box of half-eaten pizza next to him, hung out on his loft bed typing on his laptop computer. "You know what's fun?" he asked, grinning. "Instant messaging four girls at once."

Josh was still thinking about helping people. "Like one time, I made Drake come with me to volunteer at this home for the elderly," Josh said, grabbing a couple of almonds.

Drake was way more interested in having a good time. "But it was *not* fun when Josh brought me to some old folks' home to" — he grimaced and made quotation marks in the air — "help out."

"We met this couple who were in their late eighties." Josh smiled fondly. "Murray and Francine Boshwit."

Drake rolled his eyes. Talk about a bad time. "Which is where I got to meet Murray and Francine Boshwit."

"Mrs. Boshwit tried to cut Drake's hair because she thought he was a hippie." Josh laughed, remembering how Drake had totally freaked when Mrs. Boshwit pulled out her sewing scissors and started waving them around.

"Next thing I know, she's coming at me with scissors, yelling, 'Hold still, hippie!'" Drake imitated in a high, squeaky, old-lady voice.

"And then Mr. Boshwit starts telling us these stories," Josh said, cracking another walnut.

Drake typed an answer to girl number two and read girl number four's instant message, still thinking about the Boshwits. "And then her husband starts yapping about the old days," he said, shaking his head.

"Which wouldn't have been so bad, except that he was eating meat loaf while he talked." Josh made a face. Even he had to admit that it was kind of gross.

"And the whole time he's talking, he's scarfing down meat loaf." Drake grabbed a piece of pizza and took a big bite.

"It was kind of like ..." Josh grabbed a handful of nuts and shoved them in his mouth to demonstrate.

"'You give me one good reason why they should have canceled *Bonanza!*'" Drake said, imitating Mr. Boshwit. Pizza chunks dribbled out of his mouth, down his chin, and onto his clothes and laptop.

"When I was seventeen, I dated the ugliest girl in all of Wisconsin," Josh said in a shaky, old-man voice. He

spewed pieces of nuts
down his chin and across
the table with every word.

Drake shuddered at the
memory. He used to love
meat loaf. He hadn't been
able to even look at it since,
let alone eat it. "I never
went back there again,"
he said.

Josh smiled. Mr. Boshwit's
stories were kind of
funny, if you protected
yourself from the food
chunks coming at you while
he told them. And the old
guy loved having new
people around to listen to
his old stories. "Anyway, I

went back to that old folks' home a bunch of times."

"**Because instant messaging girls is way more fun than having Mr. Boshwit spit meat loaf on your face.**" Drake said, before turning back to his computer.

"Because I really like cheering up old people," Josh said with a smile.

Josh Nichols walked through the high school halls on his way to English class, looking for his stepbrother, Drake. Drake was usually easy to spot. All Josh had to do was look for a group of pretty girls. Drake would be in the middle of them. But not today. Josh hoped that meant Drake had already gone to class.

The third-period bell was about to ring, and Mrs. Hayfer hated lateness. Josh ran into class and looked around before sitting at his desk. Most of the class was already there, but Josh noticed Drake was missing. "Aw, jeez!" Josh said to himself. Drake was going to be late again.

"Ted, have you seen Drake?" Josh, mildly panicked, asked the guy in front of him.

Ted didn't hear. He was rocking out to the music on his MP3 player.

Josh tapped his shoulder and raised his voice. "Hey!"

Ted turned around. He didn't take his earphones out. He just yelled over his music. "What's up?"

Josh had to yell, too, just to be heard. "Have you seen Drake?"

"Nah, sorry," Ted said. Then the worried look on Josh's face reminded Ted of another one of Josh's problems. "Oh, hey," he said. "Did that ointment make your rash go away?"

Josh froze in embarrassment. Not only was Drake late for Hayfer's class, Ted had just announced to the whole room that Josh had a rash. He heard a few snickers.

"A little louder," Josh said sarcastically. "I don't think they heard you in Australia!"

Ted shrugged and turned around.

Andrea sat down at the desk behind Josh. "What do you need Drake for so bad?" she asked.

"I don't," Josh said over his shoulder. "But Mrs. Hayfer already hates him — if he's late one more time she's gonna be really mad."

Drake and Josh were two guys with different personalities — totally different. Josh was on time; Drake was late. Josh worked hard in school; Drake just scraped by. Drake was cool; Josh was, well, not so cool. But after Drake's mom married Josh's dad, they became not just brothers but best friends. Josh knew that Drake was there for him no matter what. Josh tried to cover Drake's back, too. But there was only so much he could do, especially if Mrs. Hayfer got to class before Drake.

And of course she did, precisely three seconds before the bell. "Good morning, adolescents," Mrs. Hayfer said, narrowing her eyes and cutting off all conversation.

The bell rang.

"Please take your seats." Her words could be taken as a polite request, but her tone of voice made it clear — that was an order. Kids rushed to their desks. "Ted, take off your headphones or I will sell them on the Internet." Mrs. Hayfer watched Ted obey her request, then narrowed her eyes again and scanned the room, searching for trouble.

Josh's eyes darted to the empty desk next to him, then away. Maybe Mrs. Hayfer wouldn't notice. But then she did.

"We have an empty seat," she said. "Who's not here?"

Two girls suddenly rushed into the classroom

looking totally upset. "Mrs. Hayfer!" one of them said. "The lunch ladies are fighting again!"

Mrs. Hayfer sighed and rolled her eyes. "What is it about sloppy joe day that makes those women so violent?" she asked. She grabbed the baseball bat she kept on hand for emergencies and rushed out of the room toward the cafeteria.

"So what are the lunch ladies fighting about?" Josh asked.

The girl, Becca, broke into a sly smile. "Oh, they're not fighting."

Josh's forehead wrinkled in confusion. Something didn't make sense. "Then why'd you tell Mrs. Hayfer that they were?"

Just then, Drake Parker swaggered into the classroom sporting his usual look — a vintage logo T-shirt, flared jeans, and a vintage jacket. "Thank you, Becca," he said, shaking his shaggy brown hair out of his eyes.

Josh threw his hands up into the air. Now he understood. "Of course," he said out loud. Drake had made up the cafeteria fight so that he could slip into class without Mrs. Hayfer noticing he was late.

"And how can I ever repay you?" Drake asked Becca.

"I think you can guess," Becca said, flirting.

Drake leaned over and gazed into her big brown eyes before breaking into a slow, dreamy smile, just for her.

Becca melted for a second, then grinned back. "Let me know if you need any more help," she said.

"Let me know if you need any more Drake," he answered, watching Becca and her friend go back out into the hall. He spotted Josh across the room and remembered something. "Oh, Josh, you left your ointment at home." He tossed his brother a tube before slipping into his desk.

Josh cringed. His face turned red. "Is nothing personal?" he shouted in complete exasperation. The kids at the desks on either side of him inched away. Andrea pulled her desk closer to the back wall. He heard more snickers in the background. Now he'd probably be called Ointment Boy or Rash Man for the rest of the day.

Mrs. Hayfer came back into the room and set her

bat down. "Well, the lunch ladies were not fighting, and I don't know why those girls called me." She scanned the room for trouble and spotted Drake. Her face tightened in contempt. "Drake Parker. Were you here when I left?" she asked.

"Oh, yeah. Totally," Drake answered with a nod. "You probably didn't see me because I had my face buried in this book."

Mrs. Hayfer didn't believe that Drake had ever buried his face in a book, and certainly not in her classroom. "Are you lying to me, Drake?" she asked.

"Would I lie to you?" Drake asked with an innocent smile.

"Let me think." Mrs. Hayfer pretended to consider for a moment. "Yes. But I know someone who never lies." She strolled to Josh's side, crossed her arms over her chest, and stared into his eyes with an intimidating expression. "Josh, was Drake on time to my class today?"

Josh started to sweat. His eyes darted from Mrs. Hayfer to Drake and back again.

Drake signaled with a slight nod. He needed Josh to back him up.

Josh wanted to stand up for Drake, but his words always got all twisted when he tried to lie. He stammered and stuttered and gave himself away the minute he even thought about lying. But he couldn't rat on his brother.

Josh decided to avoid the question altogether. "Ya know, like . . . what is *time* when you think about it?" He nervously ran his hand through his dark, wavy hair. Beads of sweat started to form under his gray button-down shirt. "Because, you know, Einstein theorized that time is actually —"

"Josh!" Mrs. Hayfer said, cutting him off. Then she leaned in and gave him an even more pointed stare, demanding an answer.

Josh turned into a puddle of panic. "No, he wasn't here on time," he said reluctantly.

"Josh!" Drake yelled.

But Josh had already started telling the truth and now he couldn't stop himself. It all poured out of him in one big rush. "He told that girl to come in here and trick you into leaving so that he could sneak into class!"

Josh knew he was in trouble with Drake now, but

he couldn't help it. Drake was the shrewd liar; Josh was the truth-teller. He only hoped Drake would go easy on him later. He turned to his brother. "I'm sorry, but I can't lie, and if you murder me in my sleep tonight I'd appreciate you doing it in a way that's not painful. Is that too much to ask?" He slumped down in his seat and hid his face in his hands.

Drake glared at him, but Mrs. Hayfer only grinned.

Drake and Josh hung back when the bell rang. They stood in front of Mrs. Hayfer's desk, waiting to hear Drake's punishment.

"Okay, how many days of detention are you going to give me?" Drake asked.

"None," Mrs. Hayfer answered coolly.

"None?" Drake was visibly surprised. No detention? He couldn't believe it. Hayfer lived to make him stay after school.

"She said none," Josh said. His voice went up in disbelief.

"I heard the none," Drake said, totally relieved.

"I'm putting you in remedial English," Mrs. Hayfer said flatly.

Remedial English? Josh gasped. But Drake's reaction was even more extreme. He jumped back in horror and screamed like a little girl. Mrs. Hayfer couldn't be that evil — not again.

"What's the matter, Drake?" Mrs. Hayfer asked,

totally enjoying Drake's panicked reaction. She liked nothing better than making Drake Parker squirm. "Did you not enjoy your last experience in remedial English class?"

Drake shuddered. The last time Mrs. Hayfer got mad at him — really mad — she had sent him to remedial English. Drake tried to block the memory, but it came flooding back to him. He remembered it took him ten minutes to find the classroom, deep in the school's basement, and he was still the first one there. Even after the room filled up, he was the only guy actually sitting at a desk. The other kids were all on their feet, throwing things, laughing, fighting, and screaming at one another.

The remedial English teacher, Mr. Talbot, didn't seem to notice that he had totally lost control of his class, even though his students had tied his arms and legs together and he couldn't move. He was still trying to teach. "Would someone like to come to the board and diagram that sentence . . . and untie me?" he asked.

Some guy who looked more like a convict than a high school student marched to the front of the room and yelled at the teacher, "Stop talking!" He had a huge dog at the end of a very short leash. It barked and snarled in agreement.

"I don't think you're allowed to have dogs at school," Drake said, watching the dog snap and drool.

The guy got right in Drake's face. "You leave Cuddles alone," he shouted.

Cuddles growled like he wanted to sink his big teeth right in Drake's neck. Drake held his hands up in surrender and the guy walked off. But just then two scary-looking twin girls took the desks on either side of him. They wore black clothes, black lipstick, black eye makeup, and had dyed their hair a matching shade of black. One had pierced eyebrows, the other had a huge silver loop through her lip, and both had nose rings. It hurt Drake just to look at them.

"I hear you're a good date," the first girl said.

"Oh, no. Not really," Drake answered. Inside he was thinking: *Yeah, with girls from planet Earth, not whatever dark world you're from.*

But the second twin didn't believe him. "You're our new boyfriend," she announced.

"I get to go out with him first," her sister yelled.

"No, I do!" said the second twin.

The girls each latched onto one of his arms and played tug-of-war with Drake as the prize. He thought they might rip him right in half. Suddenly Cuddles didn't seem so bad. "Ow, ow, ow," he yelled. "Save me, Cuddles!"

Drake shook himself out of the memory, too horrified to recall anything more about that day. He spent weeks sneaking around in the halls, trying to avoid the creepy twins. Finally, they seemed to forget all about him. But now Mrs. Hayfer was going to send Drake back, and it would begin all over again.

Mrs. Hayfer still stared at Drake, waiting for an answer. "Did you not enjoy your last experience in remedial English class?" she had asked.

"You cannot put me back in remedial English!" Drake said. He wanted to sound strong, but he could hear the terror in his voice, and so could Mrs. Hayfer.

She smiled again. She knew she had Drake exactly where she wanted him. "Well," she said slowly. "There is one other option."

Drake was immediately suspicious. "What other option?"

"I could give you a Little Sibling," she said.

Drake blinked in total confusion. "A baby pig?"

Josh and Mrs. Hayfer both dropped their heads in disgust. Could Drake really not know what a Little Sibling was?

"A sibling is a brother or sister," Josh explained.

"Yes," Mrs. Hayfer agreed. "My husband, Jerold, is a sponsor for the Little Sibling Foundation."

Drake turned from one to the other with a confused expression. "I'm almost sure siblings are baby pigs."

Mrs. Hayfer's eyes almost bugged out of her head. "Well, they're not!" she yelled.

Josh pulled Drake aside. This option was way better than remedial English. He didn't want Drake to mess it up. "Little Siblings is an organization that matches up underprivileged kids with an older brother or sister," he explained.

Okay, Drake was finally willing to believe that siblings weren't pigs. He turned to Mrs. Hayfer. "So you're going to punish me by making me babysit some kid?" he asked.

"I'm hoping it will teach you to be responsible," Mrs. Hayfer said in a stern tone of voice.

Drake turned to his brother, his eyebrows raised in a question.

Josh nodded, urging Drake to take the deal. The Little Sibling was a much better idea than the scary twins in remedial English.

Mrs. Hayfer picked up a clipboard and held it out to Drake. "It's your choice, Drake. You can either get a Little Sibling or you can go back to remedial English class. Which will it be?"

Drake didn't think either one was a good choice, but he sighed and grabbed the clipboard from her. Anything had to be better than remedial English. "I'll take the baby pig," he muttered, signing his name.

CHAPTER THREE

That Saturday Drake answered the door to an older man and a kid who looked like he was around nine years old.

"Hi, are you Drake?" asked the man.

"That's me," Drake answered.

"I'm Jerold Hayfer. My wife is your English teacher," he said.

Drake nodded. The guy looked like a total stiff — exactly the kind of man Mrs. Hayfer would marry. "Right."

Mr. Hayfer stared at Drake for a second. "She hates you."

Drake nodded again. So that proved it. Mr. Hayfer wasn't any more fun to be around than his wife was. "I know," he said.

"Well, this is Sammy," Mr. Hayfer said, putting his hand on the kid's shoulder and pushing him gently through the door. "Try not to screw him up." He glared at Drake for a second. "Later," he said, and left.

Drake watched him leave, then checked out his "baby pig."

Sammy looked up at Drake with an excited smile. "So . . ." Sammy said.

"So . . ." Drake tried to come up with something more to say, but he really had only one question. "When are you getting picked up?" he asked.

"I just got here," Sammy protested.

"Right. Well, I have some stuff for you to play with." Drake led Sammy into the living room. "Here, check it out." He pointed to a pile of old toys sitting on the dining table.

"Okay," Sammy said.

Drake picked up a red sports car. "A remote-control car," he said.

"Cool!" Sammy checked out the car. The excitement left his voice. "It's missing two wheels," he said.

"Yeah." Drake shrugged. What was he supposed to do, buy new toys? He started piling it all in Sammy's hands. "And here's a paddle thingy, and some coloring books, and a calculator, and tinfoil." Tinfoil? How did that get there? But it didn't matter. Sammy could come up with something, learn to be creative. It wasn't Drake's problem.

"Have fun," Drake said. His work was done. It was time to put his feet up and relax. He vaulted over the back of the couch and grabbed the remote.

"Wait, what are you going to do?" Sammy asked. He thought the whole point of the Little Sibling program was to spend time with his Big Sibling.

"Watch TV," Drake answered.

"Can't we do something together?" Sammy asked.

Drake rolled his eyes and sighed. This kid was seriously getting in the way of his couch time. "Like what?" he asked.

"You could help me with my homework," Sammy said.

Drake laughed. "Dude, I don't even do my own homework."

"But I need help with fractions."

Drake sighed again. It was Sammy or remedial English, he reminded himself. And he had picked Sammy. "All right. Let's take a look at your homework."

"Okay," Sammy said, taking off his backpack and

searching inside. "This week we're learning about least common denominators. Like if I want to add one-half and one-third," he explained, "I'm supposed to multiply the denominators."

Sammy was cut off by a ringing telephone. It was Drake's cell.

"Oooh, I gotta take this," Drake said, checking the screen. "Hey, Carmella," he said into the phone. "How's it going?"

Sammy put his hands on his hips. Now it was his turn to do some eye rolling. He couldn't believe his new Big Sibling was so lame.

"Oh, you do?" Drake said, laughing into the phone. "Oh, you dooooo?" he said again, laughing even harder. "Nah, I'm not busy."

Sammy held his arms up as if to say, "What about me?"

But Drake didn't notice. He had a girl on the phone. Sammy couldn't compete. "Yeah, I'd love to hear about your dream," he said to Carmella as he sat back and crossed his legs.

"Uh, hello?" Sammy said. "I still exist."

Drake didn't even look up. He held up a finger to

signal Sammy to wait. "So you were captured by pirates? Oh, right, *alien* pirates," Drake said.

Sammy wandered back over to the broken toys on the table. Drake had to be the worst Big Sibling ever. He grabbed the tinfoil and decided to take a tour of the house.

Drake still didn't notice. "They were all named Drake?" he said into the phone. "Interesting. Yeah, talk a little slower."

Upstairs, Sammy had found someone much more interesting to hang out with than Drake and his cell phone. And he'd found a use for the tinfoil. He sat on the edge of the couch in Drake and Josh's room and watched Josh pour milk into a cone of tinfoil, surrounded by newspaper.

"Now I pour the milk into my magic newspaper," Josh said, emptying the bottle and setting it down. "And say the magic word."

"Oooh, can I say it?" Sammy asked excitedly.

"Sure," Josh said. He leaned forward and whispered in Sammy's ear, "Say *Sammy-kaazam.*"

Sammy's eyes lit up. "*Sammy-kaazam!*" he shouted.

"And . . ." Josh smashed the newspaper cone down into his fist. The milk had disappeared. "Ta-daaa!"

Sammy clapped. That trick was totally cool.

Just then Drake ran into the room looking for Sammy. Fifteen minutes into Carmella's pirate story, he had noticed his Little Sibling was missing. But it took him another ten minutes to start looking for him. "There you are," he said. "What are you doing up here?"

"Hanging with Josh," Sammy said happily.

Drake frowned and pulled Josh aside. "What are you doing?" Drake asked.

"Making milk disappear," Josh answered. If Drake had ever stuck around for one of Josh's magic shows, he would know that. He was saving the never-ending handkerchief for his next trick.

"Dude, Sammy's supposed to be hanging out with me," Drake said. "You want Hayfer to stick me back in remedial English with that vicious dog and the date-starved Bartlebee sisters?"

"Sorry," Josh said. "He just wandered up here with some tinfoil, looking all bored."

Drake got defensive. "He wasn't bored," he said,

then turned to his Little Sibling and pretended to be upbeat and excited about whatever they were going to do next. "Come on, Sammy. Let's go have some fun!"

But Sammy didn't want to go. Watching Josh do magic tricks was way cooler than watching Drake talk on the phone. "I'm having fun here," he said.

"No you're not," Drake said seriously. How could hanging with Josh be more fun than hanging with Drake? "Come with me." He took Sammy by the wrist and led him out of the room.

Josh watched them go. Then he felt an odd, cold, wet sensation running down his leg. His face crumpled in disgust. He pulled up his pant leg just in time to see milk pouring out of it, into his shoe, and all over the rug.

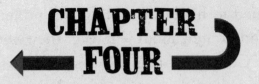

CHAPTER FOUR

Drake and Sammy sat at a café table at the Premiere, a local movie theater and hangout for the kids. Sammy was totally bored. Drake eyed a group of teenage girls at a table a few feet away. "Okay, see those girls?" he asked.

"Yeah," Sammy answered, completely uninterested.

"Okay, I say six, eight, and nine and a half," Drake said, pointing from one to the next.

Sammy looked at Drake like he was crazy. Did he really believe that girl was six? "No, they're way older than that."

Drake shook his head. No wonder Sammy needed a Big Sibling. He had so much to teach this boy. "Sammy, we're rating them on their *cuteness*."

"Well, I'm bored," Sammy said. "I'm going to go get a drink."

Drake didn't take his eyes off the girls. "Get me one," he said.

Sammy glared at Drake before heading for the snack counter. Watching Drake watch girls was lame — even lamer than the broken toys and the tinfoil. Josh's magic tricks were a lot more fun.

Just then, Josh came out of the Premiere's office, buttoning the red vest he wore when he was at work. He spotted Drake's Little Sibling. "Hey, what's up, Sammy?" he asked.

"Josh!" Sammy said with a huge smile. "What are you doing here?"

Josh grinned. People weren't usually this thrilled to see him. Well, except for Grammy, his grandmother. "Just getting ready to start my shift," he said.

"You work here?" Sammy asked. "That is so cool."

"Thanks," Josh said. "Hey, want to go check out the candy counter?"

"Oh, yeah!" Sammy said enthusiastically.

Josh led him to the concession stand. "All right. I'll give you the full tour."

"Awesome!" Sammy exclaimed.

"Go right over there." Josh pointed to a spot in front of a candy display and stood behind it. "Now

31

here we have the candy — Megathon Bar, Fluffer-nutter, Sugar Noogie." He motioned for Sammy to walk behind the counter. "Come around here. C'mon."

Sammy ran around the counter to join Josh.

Josh was getting into playing concession stand tour guide. He waved his arms around and used a TV announcer's voice. "Now right over here we have the popcorn machine, and living right next to it we've got the imitation butter dispenser. You know," he joked, "for all your synthetic butter needs." Next Josh grabbed the tube that ran from the drink machine and held it up in the air like it was the Statue of Liberty's famous torch. "And right over here we have a personal favorite of mine." He took a theatrical pause and tried to keep a straight face. "The hose of many sodas," he said dramatically, with one hand over his heart.

Sammy and Josh were having so much fun that they didn't notice Drake walk up. When Sammy didn't come back with his soda, Drake's thirst had eventually driven him to the snack counter. He wasn't thrilled to find Sammy with Josh. Again.

"Sammy? What are you doing?" Drake asked. "I'm thirsty here. Oh, and guess who just walked in? Two nines and a ten."

Sammy was fed up. All Drake wanted to do was talk to girls, talk about girls, and look at girls. "Who cares about girls?" Sammy said.

Drake gasped, totally shocked. Then he got serious. If there was one piece of Drake wisdom he could pass along to his Little Sibling, it was that girls were important — very important. "Sammy, don't ever say that," he said seriously. "Now, come on. We've got a lot to do."

"No." Sammy stamped his foot. "I want to stay here with Josh."

"What?" Drake asked.

"I want him to be my Big Sibling," Sammy said.

This was absolutely the worst moment for Mrs. Hayfer to walk into Premiere, but that's what she did. She immediately zeroed in on Drake and Sammy.

Josh saw her coming and tried to signal Drake without her knowing. "Mrs. Hayfer," he coughed into his hand. "Mrs. Hayfer."

Drake whipped around to see that his English teacher was right behind him, and her knowing smile let him know that she had heard every word of what Sammy just said. Sammy didn't want Drake. He wanted Josh.

"Mrs. Hayfer? What are you doing out . . ." Drake tried to keep the disgust out of his voice while he searched for the right words, but he couldn't. ". . . in public." As far as he was concerned, teachers belonged in one place and one place only — school. Not out in the world with normal people.

"Apparently watching you fail. Miserably," she answered with a satisfied smirk. "Josh, would you take Sammy to the nurse for a moment?"

Josh blinked. "There's no nurse here."

"To the nurse," Mrs. Hayfer ordered.

The tone of her voice was enough to terrify both Josh and Sammy. "C'mon, Sammy," Josh squealed. They both ran as fast as they could.

Drake watched them run away screaming. Mrs. Hayfer had that effect on people. He wished he could run, too. But clearly he was in trouble with her again — mega trouble. "Mrs. Hayfer, I can explain —"

She cut him off. "Drake, we had a deal. You stay out of remedial English as long as you're Sammy's Big Sibling. But if Sammy prefers Josh, well . . ." Mrs. Hayfer smiled. "I think we know what will happen to you."

Drake pictured himself back in the remedial English classroom. The Bartlebee sisters were playing tug-of-war with him, each one insisting that she would have the first date. Cuddles, the vicious dog, was just waiting for them to tear one of his arms off so he could chow down on it. The teacher was shouting for help in the background.

The whole scene nearly set Drake off on a screaming jag of his own.

He shook himself out of the horrible daydream. "Okay, okay," he said to Mrs. Hayfer, totally scared. He'd do whatever it took to be Sammy's Big Sibling. Anything to stay out of remedial English and out of range of Cuddles's snapping teeth. "Just give me one day and I promise Sammy will love me."

"Make sure it happens," Mrs. Hayfer said seriously.

Drake nodded.

She started to walk away, then turned back. "Oh, and Drake? Guess what?"

"What?" he asked.

She narrowed her eyes. "I hate you."

Drake gulped. "I know," he said. She told him all the time.

CHAPTER FIVE

The next day, Josh and Sammy hung out in the kitchen wearing matching aprons and chefs' hats while they pretended to star in their own cooking show. Fresh ingredients were spread out on the counter, and Josh had set up a camera on a tripod to record every moment of their culinary masterpiece in the making.

"Now, to make Chicken Paillard," he said, pronouncing the dish *pie-yard*, "you must first pound your chicken with a mallet."

Sammy handed Josh the kitchen tool. "Your mallet, Chef Josh."

"Thank you, Chef Sammy," Josh said, mugging for the camera.

"Now . . . pound it!" Sammy shouted.

Josh pounded the chicken like he was playing the drums while he and Sammy danced. His stepsister, Megan Parker, walked into the kitchen and grabbed an apple from the fruit bowl on the counter. She had not only messed up his carefully arranged fruit display, she had walked right in front of the camera.

"Megan," Josh whined, pressing the stop button on the remote. "You just walked through the shot."

"What are you talking about?" Megan asked, confused. She had irritated Josh completely by accident, but she couldn't pretend to be unhappy about that. Megan lived to torture her brothers — especially Josh.

"We're pretending to be TV chefs." Sammy gestured to their chef hats. Wasn't that obvious?

"Yeah, with our own cooking show," Josh said proudly, pointing to the camera.

Megan rolled her eyes. Josh was always getting excited about some dorky activity. It made making fun of him just too easy. "What's it called?" she asked. *The Iron Idiot?*"

Josh narrowed his eyes. Megan would not mock Chef Josh. "That's it! Off the set," he ordered, like a true kitchen diva.

"Whatever," Megan said, leaving the kitchen.

Josh got back into character and restarted the camera. "Now, Chef Sammy will show us our finished product."

Sammy reached below the counter and pulled out a beautiful platter of Chicken Paillard with a made-for-TV flourish. "Chicken pie-yard for six!" he announced.

Josh stuck his finger in the sauce and tasted it. "Mmm," he said with a smile. "Pie-yardy."

Sammy laughed at Josh's joke and put the platter down. "Man, you are so much fun," he said.

"Yeah?" Josh asked, a little surprised. "You, too, buddy."

Sammy could tell Josh didn't really believe him. "No, I mean it," Sammy said. "You're, like, the coolest guy ever."

"Seriously?" Josh asked, still unconvinced.

"Yeah," Sammy said, totally serious.

"Well, that's a first," Josh said. No one had ever called him "the coolest" before. Josh was the responsible guy who was nice to old people, always did his homework, and followed all the rules. Drake was the cool guy with his own band. Drake was the kind of guy other kids wanted to hang out with. Josh was the kind of guy parents and grandparents said was a nice boy.

"What do you mean?" Sammy was visibly surprised. He couldn't believe that Josh didn't know how much fun he was. And to Sammy, nothing was cooler than a guy like Josh who knew how to have fun.

"You know," Josh answered slowly, "Drake being my brother, people usually think he's the cool guy. So it's kind of nice having someone think it's the other way around for once."

Sammy smiled at his Big Sibling. Josh was not only cool — he didn't know how cool he was.

Just then, Drake rushed into the kitchen. "Josh!" he said, grabbing his brother's arm. Then he flashed Sammy a big, insincere smile. "Hey, Sammy," he said, before dragging Josh into the living room.

"I have got to talk to you," Drake said as soon as they were far enough away that Sammy wouldn't hear. "All right, listen. You have got to help me! I'm in big trouble!"

"Okaaaay," Josh agreed. He was used to this — it could be irritating, but it went along with being Drake's brother. "Whose girlfriend did you try to date now?"

Drake was totally frustrated. "I'm talking about Sammy!" Drake yelled.

Josh didn't get it. "Sammy has a girlfriend?" he asked.

Drake slapped his brother across the face — didn't he know just how important this was? Didn't he remember what Drake had gone through in remedial English? "Focus," he yelled.

"Ow!" Josh grabbed his cheek. All he could focus on was the fact that Drake had just slapped him. He slapped Drake back.

Drake slapped Josh again, sending his head to the left.

Josh slapped Drake, sending his head to the right.

Soon they were in an all-out slapping fight — four arms waving in the air, slapping at whatever they could. Josh swung too wide and hit himself on the side of the head. Drake almost fell over the coffee table. But mostly they were just slapping each other's hands, and it was totally clear that neither of them was going to win this thing.

"Time-out!" Drake yelled, jumping back out of Josh's reach.

Josh stopped slapping and tried to catch his breath. He didn't even know what they were fighting about.

Drake pulled himself together. "Now, listen!" Drake said desperately. "If Sammy doesn't want me to be his Big Sibling, then Mrs. Hayfer's going to send me straight back to remedial English!" He shuddered, thinking about what might happen. "And I will not date the Bartlebee sisters, Josh! I won't do it!"

Josh threw his hands up in the air. "What do you want me to do?" he asked. It wasn't his fault that Sammy liked him better. He was just more fun — Sammy said so.

Drake had it all worked out. It was simple. "Here's the plan," he explained with a smile. "You be mean to Sammy."

"What?" Josh yelled. How could he be mean to Sammy? That was totally out of the question. He liked Sammy. Sammy liked him. They had fun together.

"C'mon," Drake explained. "If Sammy hates you, then he'll just come running straight back to me."

Josh was speechless for a second. Drake was actually asking him to be mean to a little kid — a little kid who just happened to think Josh was the coolest person ever. Josh would do almost anything for

Drake, but being mean to Sammy was *not* one of those things. He glared at his brother through narrowed eyes. "What kind of twisted person are you?" he asked.

Drake shrugged. "Does it matter what *kind*? Don't you care about me?" he asked.

Josh had to think about that for a minute. Usually the answer was yes, but right then he wasn't so sure. This request was totally out of line. "Somewhat," he answered.

"Then be a good person," Drake said, trying to appeal to the fact that Josh liked to help people. "Go in there and make that little boy cry!" Drake pointed to the kitchen.

"I will not!" Josh answered. There was no way Drake could talk him into making Sammy cry.

Drake threw his hands up in the air. He took Josh's no as a challenge. "Okay, fine, you Little Sibling stealer. We'll just see who Sammy wants to hang out with." If Josh wanted a competition, he was going to get it, Drake thought.

"Fine," Josh said. "I've got a cooking show to finish." He headed back toward the kitchen.

"Oh, yeah, what's it called?" Drake asked sarcastically. *"The Iron Idiot?"*

Megan walked through the living room. "That's my joke," she announced.

But the brothers didn't notice. They were too busy glaring at each other.

CHAPTER SIX

That night, Sammy visited Josh at the movie theater. Josh had come up with a supercool game for them to play together. He helped Sammy to lie down on his back on the snack counter with a roll of paper towels under his head.

"Okay, Sammy. Are you ready?" Josh asked.

"Ready!" Sammy closed his eyes.

Josh took the hose of many sodas and held it over Sammy's face. He pushed a button, sending a shot of soda into Sammy's open mouth. "And your answer is?" Josh asked.

Sammy swallowed. That was easy. "Mocha Cola," he answered.

"Correct!" Josh announced. "All right, round two." He squirted another shot of soda into Sammy's mouth.

"Mountain Fizz," Sammy said.

"Correct!" Josh said again. It was time to step up

the action and make this game a little harder. "All right, lightning round." He shot three quick blasts of soda into Sammy's mouth.

Sammy smacked his lips together, tasting the different flavors. He was up to the challenge. "Um . . . root beer, ginger ale, and Diet Mocha Cola."

He was right. *"Ding, ding, ding, ding, ding!* Correct!" Josh said. He put on his talk-show announcer's voice. "Congratulations. You, my friend, have just won yourself an all-expense-paid trip to Puerto Vallarta!"

Sammy sat up on the counter, laughing. He was about to suggest they play another round when a guy in a black leather jacket and a helmet rode into the Premiere on a bright green all-terrain vehicle. His eyes popped. "Whoa!" he said.

"What's going on?" Josh asked, confused. People couldn't drive four-wheelers into the movie theater.

The guy got off the machine and took off his helmet. It was Drake. "Hey, Sammy," he said. "You like my machine?"

Sammy's face lit up. Who wouldn't? "Sure!"

"Well, hop on," Drake said with a smile.

Sammy jumped off the counter, hopped onto the

ATV, and pretended to drive. "Whoa, this rocks!" he said.

"That's right. Enjoy the vehicle," Drake answered with an evil chuckle.

Josh knew exactly what Drake was doing. He was trying to steal Sammy away. He stomped up to his brother and pulled him aside. "You must be pretty proud of yourself," he said with venom in his voice.

Drake pretended not to notice how angry Josh was. "Yeah, cool four-wheeler, huh?" he asked innocently. "I borrowed it from Trevor." He leaned forward with a satisfied grin. "Sammy luuuuuvvvs it."

"I can't believe this," Josh said, watching Sammy try on a helmet. "You think you can buy him back with this green thing?"

"Probably," Drake said. "But just in case, I also have . . ." He whipped out two tickets and walked over to Sammy. "Two tickets to the sold-out *Blaine Darvey Magical Extravaganza!*"

Josh gasped. This was too much. Drake must have paid a scalper huge bucks to get his hands on those tickets. Or charmed a pretty girl out of them. Drake knew how much Josh and Sammy wanted to see that show. They had stood in line for hours, but the tickets sold out when they were just five people away from the ticket window. Sammy was totally disappointed. Josh, too. But now Sammy was so excited, he almost jumped off the ATV. "Wow! I get to go?" he asked.

"Yep," Drake answered. "And afterward, I thought we'd go to the all-you-can-eat buffet at Jen and Barry's Ice Cream Emporium!"

Sammy couldn't believe it. This was getting better and better! "Oh my gosh!"

"Yeah, I'd ask you to come, Josh," Drake said, slipping the tickets back into his pocket. "But I know you have to work here in this boring old movie theater." He grabbed the ATV's second helmet and slipped it on. "See ya!"

Josh's shoulders slumped as he watched Drake hop on the ATV and drive Sammy out of the theater. Sammy didn't want Josh to be his Big Sibling anymore. He wanted Drake. Drake's coolness had won out again.

After work, Josh hung out on the couch in the bedroom he shared with Drake. He had hooked his camcorder up to the TV so he could watch the cooking show he and Sammy had created. Josh knew it was silly to be so upset about a little kid he had just met, but he was bummed — big time. It wasn't just that Drake had won. Josh was used to that. But he missed spending time with Sammy.

"Now, Chef Sammy will show us our finished product. . . ." Josh watched himself say.

Then Sammy had pulled out the platter they created. "Chicken pie-yard for six!"

Josh watched Sammy laugh at his dumb "pie-yardy" joke again, then smiled sadly when he heard Sammy's next line.

"Man, you are so much fun," Sammy had said.

"Yeah?" Josh heard himself ask.

Drake ran into the room, taking his jacket off and

dropping the four-wheeler helmet on his loft bed. "Hey, Josh," he said.

Josh quickly pressed stop. "Hey," he said coldly.

"Hey, man, I'm really sorry I had to take Sammy away from you. But I could not deal with remedial English," Drake said.

Josh didn't want Drake to know how upset he was. He didn't want to admit — even to himelf — how much he liked being the guy Sammy thought was cool, and how much he would miss that. "Whatever. It's cool," he said, getting up. "I'm going over to Mindy's."

"Oh, c'mon," Drake said, taking in Josh's long face. "You're mad at me."

"No I'm not," Josh insisted, but he couldn't keep the sadness out of his voice. "Sammy doesn't mean anything to me. He's just some kid. I don't even care."

Drake watched his brother leave. He knew that wasn't true. Sammy wasn't just some kid, and Josh did care about him. So why was he pretending not to? Drake noticed the camcorder on the table and pressed play on the remote. Sammy and Josh appeared on the TV, dressed up in their dorky chef hats and aprons.

"Man, you are so much fun," Chef Sammy said onscreen.

"Yeah? You, too, buddy," Josh said.

"No, I mean it. You're, like, the coolest guy ever," Sammy said.

Drake noticed the look of surprise on Josh's face. "Seriously?" Chef Josh asked Chef Sammy.

"Yeah," Sammy had answered.

"Well, that's a first," Josh said.

Then Drake watched Josh tell Sammy how everyone else thought Drake was the cool guy. He could tell how much it meant to Josh to be cool in Sammy's eyes. Drake felt cool like that all the time — *let's face it,* he told himself, *you are cool* — and he knew everybody else thought so, too. But Josh hardly ever got to feel like the coolest guy in the room. He had just confessed that onscreen. And Sammy was the one who had made Josh feel that way.

Now Drake was bummed. What had he done to Josh? He looked over his shoulder, wondering if he should stop his brother and apologize. But somehow Drake knew Josh wouldn't want to talk about this. Sometimes Drake thought it was a major pain to be compared to Josh — especially by teachers. It wasn't until he saw the tape of the cooking show that Drake thought about how hard it was for Josh to be compared to him and always come up short in the coolness department.

The next day, Sammy couldn't wait to get to the magic show. "Hey, Megan. Where's Drake?" he asked, running in as soon as Megan answered the front door.

"Over here," Drake groaned. He was lying on the couch huddled under a blanket in his pajama bottoms and a T-shirt, looking miserable. There was an ice pack on his head.

"Hey, Drake," Sammy said.

Drake took a thermometer out of his mouth to mumble a hello in a scratchy voice. "What's up, Sammy?"

Sammy was too excited about Blaine Darvey to notice Drake was sick. He bounced onto the couch. "Are you ready to go?" he asked.

"I can't," Drake said. "I'm really sick." He started to cough.

Sammy's face fell. "But we're supposed to go see the Blaine Darvey magic show. And then the ice cream buffet."

"Sorry, buddy," Drake said weakly. "I can't go. But, hey, I don't think Josh has plans." He handed Sammy the tickets. "Why don't you see if he'll take you?"

Sammy's face lit up again. "Okay," he said, taking the tickets. "Josh! Josh!"

"Hey, what's up, Sammy?" Josh asked, coming into the living room.

"You busy?" Sammy asked.

"No, I was just upstairs watching *Oprah*," Josh said, and then he caught himself. Oprah wasn't cool. Oprah wasn't something Drake would watch. "I mean football," he said in a much deeper voice.

"I love Oprah," Sammy said with a smile.

Josh got excited. "Oh my gosh, is she great or what?" Then he remembered — the Blaine Darvey show. Why were Sammy and Drake still here? "I thought you and Drake were supposed to be at a magic show."

"He's sick," Sammy said. "You want to take me?" He held out the tickets.

"Yeah, sure," Josh said. "Are you sure you're too sick to go?" he asked Drake. Josh would have had to be half dead to miss the Blaine Darvey show. And he knew if he went instead of his brother, Mrs. Hayfer might send Drake back to remedial English.

"I guess I could try," Drake said. He tried to sit up, but suddenly put his hand on his side and started to groan. He lay back down again. "Nope. I've got pancreas troubles," he said through his pain. "You guys go have fun."

That was all Josh needed to hear. "Will do," he said happily. "C'mon, Sammy, let's go!"

"You think Blaine Darvey will do the trick where he turns a sheep inside out?" Sammy asked.

Josh's voice rose in excitement. "If we're lucky!"

Sammy grabbed his coat and the guys ran out the front door.

Megan had watched the whole thing from the pass-through window to the kitchen. She didn't buy Drake's whole sick act. He was definitely not telling the truth. But why? She waited for Josh and Sammy to leave, then walked over to Drake with a suspicious expression. "Pancreas trouble?" she asked.

"Yeah, that's right," Drake said.

"You don't even know where your pancreas is," she said sarcastically.

Neither one of them heard Josh come back for his jacket.

"Yes, I do," Drake answered. He tried to picture the illustration of the human body from his biology book. It was in there in the middle along with a bunch of other gross stuff. "It's right . . . somewhere . . . in the tummy area," he said finally.

"You're not sick," Megan said.

"All right," Drake confessed, sitting up. "So I'm not sick. So?"

"So what'd you make it up for?" Megan asked.

"I don't know," Drake said with a shrug. "I just think that being Sammy's Big Sibling means a lot more to Josh than it does to me."

"So you faked pancreas trouble to make Josh feel good?" Megan asked. She couldn't believe it. Since when did Drake do something just to be nice?

"Yeah," Drake answered, a little surprised himself.
"You *are* sick," Megan said.

Josh stood by the front door, smiling. Drake wasn't sick. Drake was his brother. And he cared about Josh.

CHAPTER EIGHT

Josh and Sammy were totally mesmerized by the *Blaine Darvey Magic Extravaganza*. Not only did Blaine Darvey wow the crowd with his rockin' magic tricks and high-tech special effects, he actually turned a sheep inside out! Afterward they sampled all fifty-two flavors at Jen and Barry's Ice Cream Emporium. They ate so much ice cream that Jen and Barry were seriously rethinking the words "all you can eat."

Sammy said it was the best night of his life. The only thing missing for Josh was having his brother there. Josh wished he had the magical ability to erase Mrs. Hayfer's memory, or get her to give Drake a punishment other than remedial English.

But Josh didn't have magical powers. He'd have to find another way to help his brother.

The next morning, Drake stood in front of Mrs. Hayfer's desk, shifting nervously from one foot to the other.

"So, I understand Sammy wants Josh to be his Big Sibling." She narrowed her eyes at Drake and gave him an evil, satisfied smile. "Not you."

"Yep, that's right," Drake said, steeling himself for the worst.

"Can't say that I blame him." Mrs. Hayfer smiled again. She could hardly keep the evil glee out of her voice. "But you know what this means for you, Drake, don't you? Do you know what it means?" She was practically jumping up and down with excitement.

Drake nodded. He knew what it meant — he had had nightmares about it all night long. He even woke up Josh, and Josh slept through everything. One time Megan shaved off half his hair in his sleep and Josh never budged out of dreamland.

Later that day, Drake sat in the front row of remedial English, trying to scrunch down in his chair so no one would see him. But Cuddles was licking her chops, ready to take a big bite out of him, and the Bartlebee sisters were squeezing him like he was a Drake sandwich and they hadn't eaten in a week.

The teacher swung by his feet from the ceiling in

front of the class — back and forth, back and forth — like a giant pendulum on a grandfather clock. "Would someone please cut me down?" he begged.

But Drake was the only one listening, and he wasn't going to stand up and become Cuddles's morning snack.

The Bartlebee twins moved in even closer.

"Ready for our date, boyfriend?" asked the one with the pierced eyebrows.

"Oh, I don't want to," Drake said, cringing.

"I get to date him first!" yelled the twin with the ring through her top lip.

They started to play tug-of-war with him again, snarling and shouting at each other over his head.

"Ow, ow, ow!" Drake yelled. But no one listened to him any more than they listened to their teacher.

Suddenly Josh rushed in like he was in the middle of a huge emergency. "Mr. Talbot," he said frantically. "The principal wants to see Drake right away!"

Mr. Talbot was so surprised that someone asked his permission for something that he forgot to ask Josh to cut him down. "Very well," he answered. "Drake, you may go."

Drake jumped to his feet, totally relieved. "Yes, sir," he yelled over his shoulder. He ran to Josh — and safety. Whatever the principal wanted him for couldn't be worse than Cuddles and the twins from the dark planet.

The Bartlebee sisters glared at Josh.

"Why does the principal want to see me?" Drake asked when they reached the classroom's door.

Josh grinned. He wanted to do something nice for Drake — something as nice as what Drake did for him when he pretended to be sick — and that had won out over the fact that Josh usually couldn't lie. He had just told a whopper with a totally straight face. "He doesn't," Josh said proudly.

Drake grinned back. "I love you."

"I know," Josh answered.

They slammed the door behind them and ran down the hall together.

Brothers and best friends.

Part Two
Megan's New Teacher

PROLOGUE

Josh Nichols sat on the couch in the living room, with a basket of laundry next to him. "Okay, teachers? They're some of the greatest people in our lives," he said.

Drake Parker hung out in his bedroom, playing with some globs of clay Josh had brought home for some art project. "All right, teachers: some of the most annoying people in our lives," he said.

Josh folded a pair of red underwear while he thought about all the

great teachers in his life, then he frowned. "Except for Coach Bilbo."

"**And the worst was Coach Bilbo,**" Drake said, rolling some yellow clay into a ball. Then he smashed it, like he would have liked to smash Coach Bilbo.

"It's not that he was a bad teacher," Josh said thoughtfully, fluffing and folding his boxer shorts.

"**He was a bad teacher,**" Drake said. He rolled the yellow clay between his hands, thinking about just how bad a teacher Coach Bilbo was.

"It's just that he'd always get so angry, you couldn't understand what he was saying," Josh explained, trying to give the teacher the benefit of the doubt.

"All he did was yell — but you couldn't understand a word out of the guy's mouth!" Drake said, ripping the clay into two pieces.

"He'd be like ..." Josh imitated Coach Bilbo's big, booming voice, slurring his words to make it totally impossible to decipher them "... Josh! Come up to the board and write down some things about health."

"If I was, like, three seconds late to class, he'd be all ..." Drake garbled his words in imitation of Coach Bilbo's impossible-to-understand bark. "... Drake! What do you think you're doing showing up to my class late?"

Josh's whole face crumpled in confusion, remembering how hard he'd tried to understand — but that was completely not doable. "So I'd say, 'I'm sorry, Coach Bilbo. What'd you want me to do?'"

"And I'd be like, 'What?'" Drake would try to keep the sarcasm out of his voice, but Coach Bilbo made that totally impossible.

"And then he'd get madder and go . . ." Josh started to bark in Coach Bilbo style again, "Josh! I told you, you better get up to that board and write some things down, you understand me?" But how could he follow instructions when Coach Bilbo slurred his words like that? Josh never had any idea what it was that Coach Bilbo wanted.

"And then he'd get, like, furious and go . . ." Drake tried to translate what came next in Coach Bilbo's indistinct ramble. "Drake! I asked you why you were late to my class and I want an answer, dad-gummit!" Drake shook his head and raised his eyebrows in confusion. The guy had to be nuts.

"And the madder he got, the less I could understand him," Josh explained, shaking his head.

Drake threw his hands up in the air in frustration. "And I'd be like, 'Dude . . . what are you saying?'"

"But even though Coach Bilbo wasn't my favorite teacher, I felt sad when he finally retired," Josh said.

"I'll never forget the day Coach Bilbo finally retired," Drake said. "Kids lined up to watch him leave school."

"I'll always remember the last thing he said on his way out," Josh said.

Drake thought about Coach Bilbo's last day. "He walked through the front door of the school, looked back, and said . . ."

Josh barked the words Coach Bilbo style, sounding more like a mad dog than a teacher. "Hey, you crazy kids! Stop staring at me and get back to class!"

Drake barked the words Coach Bilbo style, sounding like a drill sergeant for pit bulls. "Hey, you crazy kids! Stop staring at me and get back to class!"

Part Two
Megan's New Teacher

CHAPTER ONE

Drake sat in front of a drum set he had assembled in the room he shared with Josh. His guitar was slung around his neck, and he was trying to play both instruments at once. He played a few chords on the guitar, then grabbed his drumsticks to give the drums a few licks. He moved back and forth from guitar to drums, but he couldn't find a way to play them both simultaneously. Having to keep picking up and dropping the drumsticks was slowing him down.

Drake knew he was a great musician, but playing guitar and drums at the same time was impossible. Instead of making music, he was just making noise. He half expected the walls to start complaining.

Before Josh moved in, Drake's bedroom had been his own private paradise. It stretched from the front of the house to the back, with exposed beams and unpainted wallboard. Drake built a loft bed under the window, bought an old couch and comfy chairs at a yard sale, and filled the walls with concert posters, road signs, and old license plates.

After Josh's dad married Drake's mom, they had added a bed for Josh. Drake wasn't exactly thrilled at first, but now he liked nothing better than kicking back on the couch, feet up on the coffee table, watching the tube or playing video games with his brother.

But right now he had the room to himself, and a problem to solve. "Okay, this is not working well," Drake said to himself, totally frustrated. Then he got another idea. Switching from guitar strings to drumsticks and back again was too hard. This time, Drake played a few chords on the guitar and hit the cymbals with his head. He moved back and forth from guitar to cymbals and back to guitar, using his head as a drumstick. But he still wasn't making anything that could be called music, and he was giving himself a massive headache in the process.

Josh got home just in time to see Drake headbang his last cymbal. He cracked up. "What are you doing?" Josh asked.

"Trying to teach myself to play drums and guitar at

73

the same time," Drake said, giving up and slipping the guitar over his head. "Man, I gotta find a new drummer for my band."

"Why?" Josh asked. "What happened to that guy Mitch?"

Josh's question totally set Drake off. He moved from frustrated to totally furious in seconds. "Who?" he spat with a disgusted expression.

Confusion crossed Josh's face. "Mitch," he said. What was this, some kind of word game?

"Oh, he quit the band so he could join his church choir," Drake snapped. "Jerk!"

Josh shook his head and scrunched his face in mock disgust, imitating his brother. "Mitch," he snarled.

Drake was too caught up in his own problems to realize he was being teased. "I know," he said indignantly. "And my band's supposed to play at the Premiere's third anniversary party next Friday night."

Now Josh's confusion was real, not put on. "Wait. My Premiere?" he asked. "Where I work?"

"Yeah, why?" Drake answered.

"Helen gave me the night off next Friday because

she said they're replacing the carpet," Josh said slowly. "I wonder why she wouldn't tell me about the party."

That was an easy question for Drake to answer. "Because she doesn't like you."

Josh snapped his fingers. "Right," he said. Then Josh remembered how happy he had been when Helen had asked him to help pick the carpet — and all she really wanted was to keep him away from the party. "Aw, man," he moaned.

"What?" Drake asked.

"I was excited about the new carpet." Josh picked up piles of carpet samples. He had taken his assignment very seriously. "I spent three hours looking at swatches!"

Drake sighed in frustration. Why was Josh going on about carpet samples when he had a *real* problem to solve? "Can we talk about my drummer issue, please?" he asked impatiently.

He didn't even want to think about the people who had auditioned in the past couple of days — a rabbi who couldn't work on Friday nights, a lady who was so scary looking that she'd frighten away all their audiences, and a guy who had gone totally berserk when Drake politely asked him to up the tempo a little. Drake needed Josh's help to figure out what to do.

The phone rang, stealing Josh's attention from the problem at hand once again. "Ah, I hate phones," Drake snapped.

"Hello?" Josh said into the phone. "Yeah, this is me. Uh-huh. Nah!" Suddenly Josh got super excited. "No! I mean yes! Thank you!" he babbled. "Yeah, I'll be there. Thank you *so* much."

Josh hung up, Drake's drummer problem completely forgotten. "I've been accepted to the TTT!" he announced.

Drake gasped. "No! Not the TTT!" he said, pretending to be just as excited as Josh.

"Yeah, the TTT," Josh said, bouncing up and down. "You don't know what that is, do you?" he asked.

"Not a clue!" Drake said, still mocking Josh's excitement.

"It stands for Tomorrow's Teachers Today," Josh explained.

Drake grimaced. *That's* what Josh was so excited about? *Teachers?* "Gross," he said.

Josh ignored his brother's disgust. "It's a program that lets people in high school teach younger kids," he said. "It's a big honor."

Drake laughed. Teaching was an honor? For him it would be a punishment. "Whatever," he said sarcastically. "So what class are you gonna teach?"

CHAPTER TWO

The next day, Josh found out all about the class he was going to teach. He went to the elementary school and followed his assigned teacher, Ms. Hunter, into her fifth-grade classroom. Josh had been up half the night planning his first lesson. He was loaded down with a box full of teaching supplies.

Megan sat at a desk in the middle of the room. Her eyes widened in disbelief and she slid down in her seat. *This can't be happening,* she thought. She must be having a nightmare. But she was awake.

"Class, say hello to your new student teacher, Josh Nachos," Ms. Hunter said.

"Nichols," Josh corrected, with a big smile. He shifted nervously from foot to foot. He had dressed up for the occasion in dark jeans and a maroon-colored button-down shirt. It said he was casual but business-like, so his students would know he was fun but not a pushover.

"Nichols," Ms. Hunter repeated in a bored voice.

Neither one of them noticed Megan put her head down on her desk and try to hide behind her hands.

"Good morning, students," Josh said. "I'm very excited that I'll be" — Suddenly he spotted his stepsister. Josh's smile got even bigger. This was going to be better than he ever imagined. "Megan?" he said enthusiastically.

Here's the thing about Megan — she loved pulling pranks on Drake and Josh, stopping at nothing to embarrass her brothers. But having Josh in her classroom could backfire on her. The last thing she wanted the kids in her class to know was that Josh the supergeek lived in the same house with her.

The whole class turned to look at Megan when Josh said her name. Megan raised her head. "I swear, I've never seen him before in my life," she said, not very convincingly.

Ms. Hunter let it pass. "Well, Josh, you certainly seem excited about your first day of student teaching."

"Yes, ma'am," Josh said, setting up his microscope.

Josh might be excited about teaching, but Ms. Hunter was excited about taking a break while he took over her class. "All right. I'll be in the teachers' lounge if you need me." She started to leave, then turned back with a warning. "Don't need me," she said in a stern voice.

She passed Drake on her way out. He was loaded down with more supplies, including a giant skeleton. "I'm just bringing my brother more teaching stuff," he explained when she glared at him.

She shook her head. This TTT kid was way too excited. It could only make her look bad. "Whatever," she said slowly.

"Hey, Josh," Drake said. "Where do you want the dead guy?"

Some of the kids gasped. A couple of them looked scared. All of them were horrified. There was a dead guy in their classroom.

"It's not a real skeleton," Josh explained to the class before answering Drake. "Just put it anywhere."

Drake dropped the skeleton on the floor, then spotted his sister. "Whoa, you got Megan's class."

Megan was waving her hand back and forth across her throat, motioning Drake to be quiet. "No," she mouthed silently.

But Drake ignored her. "We're her brothers," he told the class.

Megan rolled her eyes. "Well, don't tell them," she said, but it was too late. The entire class now knew that the new teacher was her brother. And as soon as Josh started talking, they would know she was related to a giant geek.

Josh was rattling his skeleton's bones, trying to get it onto a stand so it would hang in the front of the room.

Drake had already turned his attention to a boy named Neil in the back row who was drumming on his textbook with a couple of pencils. "Hey, are you playing 'Frozen Moon' by the Bobsleds?" he asked.

"Yeah," Neil answered. "You recognized it from the drumbeat?"

"Sure, it's an awesome tune," Drake answered. "And you're good." He wasn't joking, either — the kid was really good. Maybe, just maybe, Drake had found the answer to his drummer problem.

Josh cleared his throat. He couldn't teach if Drake stood there talking to his pupils. "Drake, I'm gonna start class now," he said. "Run along."

"One sec," Drake said, then turned back to Neil. "How long have you been playing drums?"

Neil shrugged. "I don't know. A few years."

Drake had heard enough. He had to get Neil to agree to play Friday night.

Josh started to get mad. If he was going to be a good teacher, he had to be able to control the classroom, and Drake was making that impossible. Josh didn't want to seem too strict and scare the kids, so he walked to the back of the room and tried to get rid of Drake with a joke. "Knock, knock, who's there?" Josh asked. "Drake's leaving, see ya!"

Josh tried to push Drake out the door, but he resisted. "Wait," Drake said, turning back to the drummer. "Hey, you want to be in a band?"

"I'm eleven," Neil answered, confused. Wasn't that too young to be in a band?

Drake didn't care. He needed a drummer. "Cool! Meet me out front after school. I'll pick you up!" he yelled over his shoulder as Josh pushed him out the door.

"Go!" Josh said, slamming the door behind Drake.

He ran to the front of the room. Teaching was going to be fun! He turned to the class with a big smile. "Okay, class, my name is Mr. Nichols." Josh pulled out the nameplate for his desk — he had had it specially made for this moment. "Today we're going to be learning about the atom."

A boy in the back row practically jumped out of his seat to raise his hand. "My name is Adam," he said, not waiting to be called on.

Josh chuckled. "No. I meant you'll be learning about molecular bonding. Now listen," he said, beginning to pass out big, thick books. "I'm going to be teaching you guys all kinds of cool stuff about chemistry. So you're going to need these special textbooks."

All around the room, faces fell as they got a look at the books.

Katie, a girl in the row in front of Megan, read the book's title out loud. *"Advanced Molecular Theory?"* she asked.

"This is a college textbook," Adam protested. The book was so huge, he could hardly lift it.

Josh held the book in front of him with a huge smile. "I know," he said proudly.

Megan looked at the book, then at her brother. "Yo, dork."

"Excuse me, Megan. I'm your teacher," Josh pointed out firmly. He had been practicing gentle but firm classroom control ever since he got the TTT call.

Megan rolled her eyes. Like she was ever going to treat her brother like a real teacher. "Sorry. *Mister* Dork. This stuff is, like, way too hard for us," she said.

The rest of the class all nodded and talked at once. Megan was right. They were in fifth grade, not college. There was no way they'd get college-level chemistry.

Josh ignored the protests. He had a theory about education and he was sure he would prove it as a student teacher. "Look, I believe that kids are much more capable than you're given credit for," he explained. He was sure the class would do well — with the right teacher.

A blond boy in the back row pointed across the room. "Kevin's eating glue!" he shouted.

Josh was starting to get annoyed. He wanted to teach molecular bonding, and these kids were all complaining. He snatched the glue away from Kevin.

"Don't you know you're not supposed to eat glue?" he asked.

Kevin put his head down and mumbled something Josh didn't understand. Kevin's lips were glued together.

Josh turned back to the class and his theory. "Look, all I'm saying is young kids need to be challenged. And I am Mr. Challenge," Josh said confidently.

"You said you were Mr. Nichols," said Katie.

"I thought he was Mr. Dork," Adam added jokingly.

Half the room cracked up, and the other half was about to join them. Josh was losing control of the class.

Josh had planned to be one of those cool teachers that all the kids loved, but he could get tough if he had to. It was time to get this class under control with a little tough love. "All right, watch it!" Josh yelled. "I can be quick with the time-outs! I'm just saying!"

Katie turned around and whispered to Megan so Josh wouldn't hear. "That guy's your brother?" she said in disbelief.

Megan was so embarrassed that she wanted to

crawl under her desk and not come out until fifth grade was over. "Yeah," she mumbled.

"I'm *so* sorry," Katie said.

Megan shook her head sadly. Josh had turned her into someone to be pitied, and he had only been her teacher for a few minutes. How long before he totally ruined her life?

CHAPTER THREE

Neil sat at the drum set in Drake's room finishing a mean solo while Drake watched, totally impressed. Neil had been able to handle every song Drake threw at him. He ended this one with a few fast licks, followed by a couple of cymbal crashes.

"Was that good?" Neil asked.

"Good?" Drake couldn't believe the kid even had to ask. "You're amazing. You have to play with my band on Friday night."

"Okay." Then Neil remembered a potential problem. "Wait, will it be over by nine?"

"Why?" Drake asked.

"Nine's my bedtime," Neil answered.

Drake laughed and patted Neil on the shoulder. It was time to teach this kid something about rock and roll. "Dude, you're gonna be a rock star. Rock stars don't have bedtimes."

"So when do they sleep?" Neil asked.

"When they're done rocking," Drake said, as if the answer was totally obvious. Then he got serious. "So, are you in or what?"

Neil nodded. "Sure, I'll play in your band."

"All right." Drake held his hand up for a high five. "That's my drummer!"

Neil slapped his hand. His face lit up with excitement. "Man, I can't believe I'm a real rock star!" he said. He heard a horn honk out front. "Uh-oh, that's my mom." Neil grabbed his drumsticks and his jacket and started to leave. He passed Josh on his way out. "Hi, Mr. Nichols," he said.

"Hello, Neil. Don't forget to do your homework tonight," Josh said.

Neil grinned. "Drake says rock stars don't do homework. Bye!"

Josh watched Neil run down the stairs, then turned to his brother and narrowed his eyes. No homework? "Does it give you pleasure to poison the minds of children?"

"I wasn't poisoning his mind, I was just —" Drake's defense was cut off when Megan ran into the room without knocking on the door and started poking around. "Megan, what are you doing in our room?" he asked.

"Looking for my Pentendo G-S," Megan said, walking over to Josh's desk.

Josh couldn't believe it. He had given an enthusiastic and enlightening lecture that afternoon about how important it was to do homework first and play games second.

There was no way Megan could have finished all her homework by now. So why was she looking for her game? "Video games? Shouldn't you be doing something else right now?" he asked.

"Shouldn't you be trimming that giant hair sticking out of your nose right now?" Megan asked sarcastically.

"Oh, I'll get it." Drake reached over and yanked the hair right out of Josh's nose.

"Ow!" Josh screamed. "I'm not for plucking," he told his brother.

Megan spotted her handheld video game. "Oh, there it is." She turned it on and started playing, her eyes fixed on the screen, as she started to leave the room. But Josh snatched it out of her hand. "Give me my Pentendo G-S!" Megan yelled.

"No. You should be doing your homework," Josh said firmly.

"I'm not doing that homework," Megan answered just as firmly.

"Heh?" Josh asked. How could he prove his theory if Megan was refusing to do her homework? That wasn't part of Josh's plan. Plus, it would make him look bad.

"None of us are doing it. It's way too hard," Megan announced.

Now Josh was mad. If Megan thought she could get away with stuff just because she was his sister, she was wrong. And it sounded like she was getting the whole class to get in trouble along with her. "Look, little girl. I am your teacher and you will show me some respect," Josh insisted.

Megan nodded and eyed him coolly. He wasn't her teacher at home. At times like this, she thought, it was good that she knew Josh well enough to know that he didn't wear a belt. She didn't say a word. She didn't have to. She just reached out, grabbed hold of the belt loops on his jeans, and yanked them down, exposing Josh's plaid boxer shorts. *How's that for respect?* she thought.

Josh's jaw dropped. Had Megan really just done that — to her *teacher*?

Megan snatched her Pentendo G-S out of his hand and stormed out of the room.

Drake cracked up. "You got pantsed!"

Josh sighed and pulled up his pants with as much dignity as he could muster.

The next day, Josh walked into Megan's classroom dressed up like the scientist Albert Einstein. He wore a wig with gray hair that stuck straight up in the air, a gray mustache, and a coat and tie. It was all part of his plan. He would be the fun teacher that everybody liked, and his class would want to do their homework and learn all they could because of it.

"Good morning, children," he said in a German accent. "*Guten tag.*"

Megan rolled her eyes and sighed. It was hard to believe, but Josh was going to be even geekier than he was the day before. "Aw, man," she moaned.

"Who are you?" Neil asked.

"Ahhh, you must guess," Josh said, still in his German accent. "I am a very famous person. Now, who am I?"

Katie took in Josh's dusty wig and old coat. She raised her hand. "A hobo?" she guessed.

"No. Hobos aren't famous. Here's a hint. I am a famous scientist," Josh answered.

Neil raised his hand and guessed the first name that came to mind. "Harry Potter?" he asked.

"No," Josh said in his German accent. "Harry Potter is a wizard. Now think," he said, taking in the whole room. "I am a German scientist."

"A hobo?" Adam guessed.

Josh threw his hands up the air. *What's with the hobo guesses?* he wondered. "Dude, I'm Albert Einstein," he said, forgetting the accent. "You should know that from your homework last night!"

"I told you we weren't doing it," Megan said.

Josh hadn't really believed Megan the day before. He was sure the rest of his students would do their homework. "Okay, wait a minute," he said, his forehead wrinkling. "None of you did your homework?"

The kids all eyed one another nervously. No one wanted to speak up. Finally Katie raised her hand. "I tried to," she said slowly. "But I couldn't figure it out, so I asked my mom to help me."

"And?" Josh asked, relieved. At least Katie had tried to do her homework, with her mom's help.

Katie cringed. "She couldn't figure it out, either. So she asked my dad. Then he got mad and they had a big fight."

"Well, all right," Josh said slowly, wondering what to do. Then he remembered what his teachers always did to make sure the class did its homework. It was more important to be a good teacher than a fun one. And good teachers sometimes had to get tough. "Then I guess I'm going to have to give you all a pop quiz," he said.

The class erupted in a chorus of "What! No way!" and "Aw, man!" But Josh ignored them.

"Yo, Einstein," Megan said. "If you give us a quiz on homework we didn't do, we're all going to fail."

Josh wasn't swayed. "Well, maybe you all should have thought of that when you weren't doing the homework," he said, dropping a stack of quizzes on the desks in the front row to be passed back.

Katie handed the papers to Megan and narrowed her eyes. "Your brother's getting on my nerves," she said.

She wasn't the only kid who was mad at Megan. Other kids were nodding in agreement.

"He's bugging me, too," Adam told Megan.

"It's not my fault," Megan said. But she was guilty by association. If the kids were this mad at her on Josh's second day of teaching, she wondered, what would happen by the time he finished?

At least Josh's time for the day was almost over. Ms. Hunter came back to the class. "All right, children," she said, and then spotted Josh in his Einstein costume. "Oh, no," she yelled and ran back into the hall. "Security! We've got another hobo in the classroom!"

Josh looked around, confused. Another hobo?

A security guard rushed in with a can of pepper

spray and got Josh right in the eyes with the burning liquid.

"No! No!" Josh screamed. "I'm not a hobo! Stand down! Stand —" But then it was Josh who was down — on the floor. The burning in his eyes kept him from seeing the smiles on his students' faces.

CHAPTER FOUR

After school the next day, Josh worked behind the counter at the Premiere. The café had been decorated for a birthday party with balloons and streamers. When Josh realized the party was for Katie from his class, he was tempted to go over and ask if they had all done their homework. But Josh's manager, Helen, had her eye on him. So Josh stayed put.

Megan came in with Drake, holding a big, brightly wrapped box. "There's Katie," Megan said.

"Have fun at the party," Drake said. Then he spotted the big birthday cake and grabbed Megan's wrist before she could run off. "Hey, snag me some cake," he said.

Megan rolled her eyes, twisted her wrist free, and ran over to Katie's party. "Hey, guys," she said to a couple of her friends.

They turned their backs on her without even saying hello. In fact, the whole party got really quiet and looked away as soon as Megan walked up. Katie turned around and pretended not to see her.

Megan stopped for a minute. What was going on? Then she stood a little straighter and walked up to her friend. "Happy birthday, Katie," Megan said with a big smile.

Katie turned around slowly. "Oh. Hi, Megan," she said awkwardly.

"I think you're going to love this," Megan said, holding out the present.

But Katie didn't take the present. She put her hands on her hips and chewed her lip. "Umm . . . didn't you get my text message?" Katie asked.

Megan blinked in surprise. "What text message?"

"The one where I *un*invited you to this party," Katie said.

Now Megan was totally confused. "Why would you uninvite me?" she asked.

Neil stepped next to Katie. "Because nobody wants you here."

"Yeah, why don't you go hang out with your brother the teacher?" Adam said. The kids around him nodded in agreement. They looked angry.

Megan's face fell. Her shoulders slumped. She realized that everyone hated her. And she realized whose fault that was. She put Katie's present down and turned toward the concession counter. Her eyes narrowed when she saw the reason for her sudden unpopularity — her brother Josh. The supergeek had ruined everything. And he had given Megan her first — and last — F.

She stormed over to the snack counter. "Everyone hates me because of you!" she snapped.

Drake stepped back. "I wanted one piece of cake," he protested.

But Megan didn't take her eyes off Josh. "Not you. Him. Professor Dorkstein," she said through clenched teeth.

"What are you talking about?" Josh asked.

"I just got thrown out of a party because you gave us a pop quiz that we all failed," Megan said.

Drake couldn't believe it. Megan failed a quiz? Cool! "All right, you failed a quiz?" he held his hand up for a high five. "Welcome to my club."

Megan glared at Drake. "I don't want to be part of your F club," she spat.

"Well." Drake pretended to be offended and walked a few steps away, but he was close enough to listen as Josh tried to defend himself.

"Look, Megan," Josh said. "If you kids would just apply yourselves —"

Megan cut him off. He was throwing college-level work at them. News flash! They weren't in college. "We're in fifth grade!" Megan yelled. "Why don't you teach on someone your own size?"

Drake tried to help his brother out. "Oh, come on," he said to Megan. "Give him a break. He's just trying to help you guys learn something, or something." Actually Drake wasn't quite sure what Josh was trying to do, but life at home was easier when Megan and Josh weren't at each other's throats. Megan had a bad habit of getting her revenge in the middle of the night, and Drake didn't want his sleep interrupted by Josh's screams.

Just then Neil spotted Drake. "Hey, Drake," he said, leaving the party for a minute.

"Neil! What's up, my drummer?" Drake held out his fist for a knuckle touch.

"Listen," Neil said sadly. "My mom won't let me

play in your band because I failed Mr. Nichols's quiz. Sorry." Neil hung his head and went back to the party.

Drake turned around and glared at his brother. Messing up Megan's social life was one thing, but *Mr. Nichols* had just ruined Drake's band, and he had a gig in a few days.

"Look, I am a teacher," Josh said, turning from Megan to Drake and back again. "Now, I realize these kids may think I'm too tough on them, but deep down, I know they appreciate me."

"Yeah," Megan said sarcastically. "That must explain the Josh piñata."

The three of them looked over at the birthday party. Katie was blindfolded and had a big stick in her hand. She was using it to batter a giant papier-mâché piñata that looked a lot like Josh. The rest of the kids cheered each time she whacked him with her stick.

"I want to hit him," Neil shouted.

"Let me hit him. Let me hit him!" Kevin said.

"My turn!" yelled Neil.

Josh's jaw dropped as he watched his students fight for the chance to whack his head off. Katie took a big swing and landed a shot right in the middle of his neck, sending the Josh head flying across the Premiere.

It landed right in Josh's hands. His students were fighting over the chance to rip his body to shreds. Drake and Megan were both furious with him. And Josh would never be able to prove his challenging education theory if his class didn't start doing their homework.

Josh didn't know what to do, but he had to admit the artist who had made his poor, battered head had done a good job. He held it up next to his face. "It does look like me," he said.

CHAPTER FIVE

The next afternoon, Megan sat on the couch next to Drake, thinking about the fact that having Josh for a teacher had turned her into a complete and total outcast at school. "Stupid student teacher program," she muttered.

Drake sat next to her with a jar of peanut butter and some celery sticks. He crunched down on a stalk, thinking about the fact that Josh's student teacher job had cost him a drummer. "I hate student teacher programs," he agreed, then offered Megan one of his snacks. "Peanut butter and celery?"

Megan sank her teeth into the celery stick, pretending it was Josh's head. "You know, nobody in my class likes me anymore, all because of Josh. We played dodgeball in gym today. Do you know how many balls I had to dodge?"

"No," Drake answered.

"A lot of balls, Drake." Megan shuddered. Her legs

were still tired from all the running and dodging. At least when the class attacked Josh, they went after a piñata imitation. Those dodgeballs were flying at the real Megan.

"You think that's bad?" Drake asked. "Because of Josh, I have no drummer." He'd have to give up Friday night's gig, or start playing drums with his head again. His head hurt just thinking about it.

Josh came into the room, sipping a drink. "What's up, guys?"

Megan and Drake looked at Josh, then at each other. Did Josh actually expect them to speak to him, after what he had done to them?

"Hey, you hear something?" Megan asked Drake.

Drake played along. "Hmm, sort of," he said. "Kind of like an annoying buzzing sound."

"Yeah," Megan agreed. "Annoying and . . ." She pretended to search for a word, but she had a favorite way to describe Josh, and she used it at every opportunity ". . . dorkish."

"Fine," Josh said, putting his glass down and standing tall. "You guys want to play it that way? It doesn't bother me. Because I know I'm doing the right thing. I am a good teacher because I chall —" Josh was cut off when a peanut-butter-covered celery stick flew through the air and landed on his face.

Drake tried not to crack up while Josh pretended that having a celery stalk glued to his face with peanut butter wasn't strange.

"I don't care," Josh said, trying to look and sound dignified. "I like it on my face."

Drake jumped to his feet, totally fed up. "All right, Josh! You are going to change Neil's grade to an A so he can play with my band Friday night!"

Josh pulled the celery off his face. Was Drake actually ordering him to give Neil a grade he didn't earn? Josh would never be that kind of teacher.

"And you're going to stop *challenging* all my friends in class," Megan added, standing next to Drake.

"No!" Josh insisted. "You kids need to be challenged." Then he turned to his brother. "And I tell you what! I am going to whip those little kids' brains into shape! You'll see," he said, pointing at his siblings. "You'll all see!" Josh swept out of the room and into the kitchen, but his dramatic exit was marred by the fact that he forgot his punch — and he was thirsty.

Josh backed into the living room like it was the most normal thing in the world and picked up his glass. "I want my punch," he said, still trying to sound dignified.

As soon as Josh was out of the room again, Drake turned to Megan. "So, now what are we going to do?"

Megan crossed her arms over her chest and smiled. She had an idea!

"Oooh, I like that smile," Drake said. "That's a smile full of evil."

"Is there any other reason to smile?" Megan asked, with a sly expression.

Drake's eyes lit up. No one did revenge better than Megan. "You have a plan," he said. "Tell me your plan."

"Well . . ." Megan said slowly. "Tomorrow, Ms. Hunter's going to watch Josh and evaluate his teaching skills."

"Aha!" Drake said, grinning. Then realized he didn't know why that was a reason to smile. "I don't understand why that helps us."

Megan rolled her eyes. "Just get your car keys," she ordered.

CHAPTER SIX

Drake hoisted himself up the rope he had managed to attach to the school's roof. He was finally outside of Megan's dark classroom and used a credit card to unlock the window latch before opening the window and climbing inside. He was dressed in black from head to toe to avoid detection.

"Okay, Megan, I'm in," he whispered, leaning out of the window and throwing the rope down to her.

"Yeah, me too," Megan said, coming through the classroom's door. She was dressed all in black, too, and carried a silver briefcase.

Drake fell against the window, surprised and confused. "How did you get in here?" he asked.

Megan shook her head. Why was he making everything so complicated? "I walked through the front door. It's a school, Drake. Not a bank," she said sarcastically.

Drake shrugged off her sarcasm — climbing up

that rope and through the window made him feel like an undercover spy. "Whatever. Just do your thing."

Megan opened her high-tech silver case. Inside were all kinds of electronic devices. Some of them blinked and beeped. All of them looked expensive.

Drake whistled in appreciation. "How much allowance do Mom and Dad give you?" he asked.

Megan was all business. "Just be my lookout," she ordered.

Drake stood at the door while Megan got to work. She selected a pair of pliers and walked over to the sink. After working on the faucet for a few seconds, she heard a satisfying clunk. She had listened to Josh rehearsing the lesson he would try to teach in front of Ms. Hunter and knew exactly what he had planned. She substituted one of the jars on the science table with an identical-looking liquid from her case. She was about to move on when she noticed that Drake wasn't scanning the hall for signs of the janitor like he was supposed to.

"What are you doing?" she asked, totally annoyed.

Drake was using his flashlight to make shadow

puppets on the wall. "Look," he said, pleased with himself. "It's a bunny."

Megan shook her head. Didn't he know they were on a mission? "Stop that," she ordered. And then she went back to work. Operation Sabotage Josh was going to be a huge success. It had to be.

CHAPTER SEVEN

The next day at school all Megan had to do was wait for Josh to do his thing. The rest had been taken care of. She sat at her desk by herself — no one was talking to her — while the rest of the kids got ready for science. She knew they'd be friends again once Operation Sabotage Josh was in motion. She would let it slip that it was all her idea.

"Josh Nichols," Ms. Hunter said, coming into the room. "Are you ready to be evaluated?"

Josh was making some last-minute notes on his laptop computer. "Yes, ma'am," he said, standing.

"Please begin."

"Children, please take your seats," Josh said, clearing his throat nervously.

The kids all sat while Josh looked on proudly. He nodded to Ms. Hunter as if to say, *see what a good teacher I am?* but all she did was give him a weak smile. Getting kids to sit down wasn't teaching — getting them to learn was.

"Okay," Josh said, opening his laptop. He had a very special lesson planned for his evaluation. He wanted to be the best student teacher that Ms. Hunter had ever seen. "Today we're going to talk about the three states of matter: solids, liquids, and gases," Josh said, clicking a button on his laptop. "Now, I've set up a video presentation for you to watch on this monitor."

The entire class checked out the TV monitor, while Josh faced them. Megan had a sly grin on her face.

"Onscreen you can see the loosely packed atomic structure of a liquid," Josh said. But what Josh didn't know was that Megan had made a slight change in his video. Instead of the atomic structure of a liquid, the class saw two clowns slapping each other with rubber chickens. They all cracked up.

"Okay." Josh laughed, still unaware that his video had been switched. "Now, I realize this is enjoyable, but —" Josh got a look at the TV screen and did a double take. This wasn't his presentation! "What the —?"

"Why are those clowns hurting each other with chickens?" asked David.

"Yes, Josh. Why?" Ms. Hunter asked.

Josh quickly turned off the TV.

"Strike one," Megan said to herself.

"I'll move on to my next segment," Josh said nervously, trying to ignore Ms. Hunter's stern expression as she made notes on her clipboard. "Now, water is one of the few compounds that can assume the form of either a solid, liquid, or gas." He picked up a glass beaker and crossed to the sink. When Josh turned on the faucet, water shot all over the place, drenching him, the wall, and the floor. He tried to use his hands to stop the flow, but it was no use.

"This would be the liquid," Josh said weakly. He tried to pretend like nothing had happened, but that was hard to do when you were getting completely soaked.

"You broke the faucet!" Ms. Hunter yelled.

"I didn't mean to! Here, I'll fix it," Josh said, picking up the piece that had come loose. Josh stumbled around, trying to fix the sink.

"No, move!" Ms. Hunter yelled, pushing him out of the way. "I'll fix it."

Josh felt helpless watching Ms. Hunter get soaked while she tried to stop the flow of water. Then he spotted an umbrella in the corner. He opened it and held it over Ms. Hunter's head to try and keep her dry while the class cracked up even harder.

Finally, Ms. Hunter was able to stop the water. Totally wet and totally irritated, she snatched the umbrella from Josh's hands and threw it back on the floor.

"Strike two," Megan said with a smile.

Josh was completely flustered but he tried to press on with his lesson. "Next," he said.

"Oh, great," Ms. Hunter said sarcastically. "There's more."

Josh's voice was shaking when he moved behind the chemistry table. "I will now show you all how a liquid and a solid can be combined to form a gas." He picked up the bottle of liquid that Megan had switched with one of her own the night before. "Okay, first I will take this beaker of sodium sulfide and put it into this jar, which contains ten grams of carbon zeenite."

Megan had a big smile on her face. She knew what was going to happen next, but Josh had no idea what was coming.

The color of the liquid changed from pink to yellow as Josh poured it into the jar with the carbon zeenite. "Now, note how the color changes when I pour the sodium sulfide into the —"

But more than the color changed. The beaker exploded! Megan and her classmates were thrown back when a flash of light and smoke blasted into the air. There was a black cloud of smoke over Josh's and Ms. Hunter's heads. Their faces were covered in black soot. Wisps of smoke rose from the tips of their hair — which was standing straight up.

Josh waited for a long, awkward minute, trying not to cry. His hands shook and his voice wobbled, but he tried to finish his lesson. "Next . . ." he said weakly.

But as far as Ms. Hunter was concerned, Josh was finished. The steam coming from her head might have been from her boiling rage instead of the explosion. She pointed to the classroom door, screaming, "Leave!"

Josh didn't have to hear that twice. He ran out of the room. He had been totally and completely done in.

Megan slammed her college-level chemistry book closed and sat back with a satisfied smile. "Strike three and you're out," she said.

The Premiere was totally decked out for its Friday night party. Silver streamers hung from the ceiling. A glittery THIRD ANNIVERSARY banner covered one wall. The café area had been decorated with stars and balloons and turned into a stage for Drake's band.

Drake finished up a great, hard-rocking song with Neil on the drums. The audience whistled and clapped.

"Thank you," Drake said into the microphone. "How about a hand for eleven-year-old Neil Kramer on drums!"

Neil waved his drumsticks to more cheering and clapping. He was getting into this whole rock-star thing.

"Okay, we're going to take a short break," Drake said, taking off his guitar. He turned on the Premiere's stereo system and crossed over to Neil. "Great job. Thanks for playing, man."

"Thank Megan," Neil said. "If she hadn't gotten

your brother fired, I wouldn't have gotten my grade changed."

"Hey, who do you think helped her sabotage Josh's presentation?" Drake asked. He wanted some of the credit, too.

"She said all you did was drive her there," Neil said.

Drake had to admit that was true — but there was more to it. "And home," he added.

Helen, the Premiere's manager, ran over to let Drake know how much she enjoyed the set. "Drake Parker, your music makes me want to wiggle till I giggle," she said, showing him both the wiggle and the giggle.

"Thanks, Helen," Drake said. Then he braced himself for what always came next — one of Helen's huge, smothering bear hugs.

"Look at you, all cute with your microphone, like a little rock star. Oh, gimme a hug." Helen reached out and locked Drake in a bear hug, lifting and shaking him like a stuffed toy.

She set Drake down and turned to Neil. "You, too, little drummer boy."

Neil was squashed in Helen's arms. He couldn't breathe. "Is this what you meant by having girls all over you?" he asked.

Drake shrugged. "Sort of." He mostly pictured younger, cuter girls in that scenario, but now wasn't the time to explain.

Across the theater, Josh trudged out of the men's room with a plunger over his shoulder. He'd had a rotten week. First he had lost his teaching job. Then Helen told him he could come to the party, only to put him on bathroom duty when he got there. He had faced floods, explosions, and clogged toilets all in one day.

Megan and some of her classmates walked up to the concession stand. "Hey, Josh," Megan said.

Katie, David, and Adam, along with a few other former students, nodded and said hello to him, too.

Were they here to dump more abuse on him, Josh wondered? But no one glared at him. No one complained about homework or pop quizzes or grades. No one pointed and laughed. Josh was completely surprised. "What do you guys want?" he asked.

"To give you a present," Adam said.

Katie handed Josh a gift wrapped in crumpled newspaper with a big red bow on top.

Josh's forehead wrinkled in confusion. "You guys got me a present?" he asked.

"Yeah," Katie answered.

"I wrapped it," David said proudly as the newspaper started to fall away.

Josh pulled the newspaper all the way off and let it drop to the floor. Now he was even more confused. "A trophy with a giraffe on it?" he asked.

"The trophy store was out of people," Megan explained.

Josh still didn't understand. This was getting more and more bizarre.

"Read what it says," Adam told him.

Josh read the inscription. "To Mr. Nichols, our favorite teacher." Josh looked up, more puzzled than ever. "I don't get it." Suddenly he realized the present could be a trick. Maybe they were still trying to get back at him for all that chemistry homework. He quickly dropped the trophy on the counter and jumped back. "Is that gonna blow up?" he asked nervously.

"No," David said.

"Because of you," Megan explained, "Ms. Hunter quit teaching."

"Forever," Adam added.

"And we hated Ms. Hunter," Katie chimed in.

"Wait," Josh said. "I thought you hated me."

"We do," David said matter-of-factly.

"We hate you both," Katie said. "But in different ways."

The class did hate Josh's college textbook that was way over their heads, and they hated his too-hard homework, and they especially hated his pop quiz. But they also knew that Josh liked them and was really trying to teach them something. Ms. Hunter was one of those teachers who had stopped liking kids a long time ago. She was just going through the motions to collect a paycheck. She never did anything fun. Compared to her, Josh really wasn't so bad. Now that he was gone, anyway.

"Anyway, you want to come have some pizza with us?" Adam asked.

"And listen to Drake's next set?" Katie added.

Josh was still confused. "All right, you guys hate

me," he said, trying to figure it all out. "But you want me to come hang out with you?"

"Dude, we hate you as a *teacher*," David said.

Adam agreed, "Yeah, but as a guy, you're almost cool."

Megan had to keep herself from smiling. No way did she want Josh to know that she agreed with Adam. But now that Josh wasn't her teacher anymore, she was almost happy to have him as a brother.

Josh wouldn't have been able to keep himself from smiling if he wanted to. He turned to Gavin, one of his colleagues behind the snack counter. "They think I'm cool," he said proudly.

"I heard *almost*," Gavin said.

Josh didn't care. He'd take almost cool over worst teacher any day. He was going to take a break and eat some pizza with his former students.